Six Short Stories

By

Patricia A Perry

Copyright © 2020 by Patricia A Perry

All rights reserved. No part of this publication may be reproduced, stored in any form of retrieval system or transmitted in any form or by any means without prior permission in writing from the publishers except for the use of brief quotations in a book review.

Table of Contents

The Minibus 5
Chapter One: Forgotten 6
Chapter Two: Second Chance 7
Chapter Three: A New Lease of Life 8
Chapter Four: The Final Days 9

The War Babies 11
Chapter One: The Beginning 12
Chapter Two: The Sad Times 14
Chapter Three: The Farm 16
Victory in Europe! 18

The Stray Cat 19
Chapter One: Dolly 20
Chapter Two: Elsie 21
Chapter Three: Matilda 24

The Favourite Chair 27
Chapter One: Grandpa Joe 28
Chapter Two: Grandma Doris 30
Chapter Three: The Icing on the Cake 32
Chapter Four: The Final Days 33

The Red Bicycle 35
Chapter One: Matilda 36
Chapter Two: Alfie 38
Chapter Three: Daisy 40

The Peg Story 42

Chapter One: The Peg Story 43
Chapter Two: A Reprieve 45
Chapter Three: The Final Days 47

The Minibus

Written by Patricia Perry

20th of May 2020

8 weeks of lockdown

Enjoy!!!

Chapter One:
Forgotten

In a dark corner of the huge depot, stood a lonely old minibus.

He was thinking about his good old days, when he was used every day, picking up and dropping off all his passengers, young and old, all over town, at shops, schools, or wherever they needed to go and he loved it!

He felt loved, needed and appreciated, and was very happy!

Then the bus company began to get new bigger fancy buses, and slowly but surely, the minibus got used less and less, until finally, almost two years ago, he got parked up in the corner and left!!

Fair enough, he was undercover, protected from the harsh British weather, but he sadly missed the lack of sunlight and the bright faces of his passengers.

Then one day, he heard voices. He recognised them as being Albert, the company director, and Jack, the head mechanic

This made the minibus anxious, as he thought, 'this is it…my days are over'!

Chapter Two:
Second Chance

"Give me your honest opinion, Jack," the minibus heard Albert say. "I need you to have a good look at everything to decide whether the minibus should go or stay."

"Ok, boss," said Jack. "Leave it with me. I'll get back to you in a couple of hours!"

Then Jack got to work, his overalls on, and the first impression was that the bus looked alright. He stepped inside the bus and felt a strange feeling.

In his ten years as a bus mechanic, he had never felt this... It was as if the bus was talking to him! A loving, peaceful aura came over him!

He proceeded to lift the bonnet to have a good look at the engine, and was pleasantly surprised at what good condition it was in!

The tyres, apart from one, were in an okay condition as well, as were the doors, windows and seats.

Jack decided he would service the engine; after all, water and oil were a necessity for any bus!

Then he put on a new tyre, and gave the bus a jolly good clean, inside and outside.

The end result was amazing! The minibus scrubbed up well, and Jack decided there and then that the bus should stay!

Chapter Three:
A New Lease of Life

The minibus was back on the road. However, he was not about town as previously; instead, he was given a country route!

He was given a semi-retired driver called Stan. Stan had driven big buses for over 20 years, so when he told his wife, Peggy, he was going to be driving a minibus around the country lanes, she didn't think he would like or enjoy it!

However, it turned out to be the best job he'd ever had, and he loved his little minibus. He even gave it a name - Daisy!!

Stan would chat to Daisy all the time; it was good to get a word in edgeways!

They drove out to remote areas to pick up elderly passengers who needed to go shopping, or whatever, and children who needed to get to school. Stan was a cheery chap who, when he wasn't chatting to Daisy, would chat away to his passengers, and because they were the same people most days, he got to know them very well.

They would tell Stan about any worries or problems they had and Stan (and Daisy) became advisors or agony aunts (or uncles)!

Stan and Daisy were as happy as Larry, as they both felt they had been given a new lease of life.

Chapter Four:
The Final Days

Although Stan loved Peggy dearly, he was also very happy to go to work each day and be with Daisy.

He didn't even see it as a job, after the stressful days of driving his big bus around the towns and cities.

He adored the countryside. However, in his younger years, he had never really had the time to enjoy and realise that.

Above all, it was his relationship with Daisy, his cute little minibus, that he loved the most!

It was almost as though the bus had a soul.

He could not imagine a life without it now, and worried what the future held for both of them when they were ready to retire completely!

He needn't have worried; they had a good seven years together, thanks to Stan's tender loving care. He always made sure the bus had oil and water etc., and was kept spotlessly clean, inside and out. It turned out to be his pride and joy. All Stan's passengers loved them both and looked forward to their trips out, wherever that may be!

One day, as they were taking a break, Stan spotted a little bungalow for sale, with nice gardens and a driveway.

He had a chat with Peggy, and together, they decided to sell their family home and settle down for their final years in this lovely bungalow in the country!

Luckily, after the sale of their big house, there were sufficient funds left over for a rainy day!

However, Stan had other ideas. With Peggy's blessing, he purchased the minibus from his employer, Albert, for a very good price indeed.

He continued to use Daisy for a while, still picking up passengers, but for his own little business!

Then one day, Stan realised that Daisy was not driving as she could. It seemed that all the hard work had eventually caught up, and the minibus's days were over. What was he going to do?

He couldn't bear to have Daisy sent to the scrapyard, so, he had a brainwave!

He parked the minibus in his garden and painted flowers, butterflies and bees all over Daisy, in pretty colours. He and Peggy loved it!

It was a real talking point all over the village, and people would drive out just to look at it and admire it!

Stan even let the children play in it! Kiddies would squeal with delight, pretending to be not only bus drivers, but all sorts of things!!

Daisy was whatever the children's imagination wanted it to be! They had hours of fun, which made everyone, especially the little minibus, so very happy!

They could not think of a better way to spend their final days!!

The end

The War Babies

Written by Patricia Perry

Original idea by Patricia Perry

15th May 2020

Still in lockdown

Chapter One:
The Beginning

Betty's screams could be heard from the other side of Bolton as she pushed her twin sons, Alfie and George Junior, into the world!

They each had a good pair of lungs, and you definitely knew they had arrived!!

They were very lucky not to have been born in an air-raid shelter, as it was 1939 and England had been at war for a few months!

Grandma Doris was delighted with the birth of her grandsons.... She was about to play a big part in their lives!

Betty's husband, George Senior, had given his job up to join the army and fight for his country.

This made Betty both happy and sad.... She was very proud of him; he made a good soldier... but she was sad because she missed him so very much, and, he missed the birth of his sons. Neither of them knew when George would get to meet Alfie and Georgie!

Because most of the men were at war, it meant that the women, including Betty, were needed to go out to work in the factories.

So, when the babies were only two months old, Grandma Doris looked after them while Betty went to work in an ammunition factory, making bullets for the soldiers.

It was long hours and very hard work, but everyone had their bit to do for the war; no-one knew when it would end.

However, Alfie and Georgie thrived under the care of Grandma Doris, and she adored them!

Her husband, Grandpa Ted, had passed away just before the war started. She was beside herself with grief, so the boys coming into the world gave her something to focus on... a reason to go on living!

Chapter Three:
The Farm

After Doris's funeral, Betty realized she would have to return to work, in order to pay the rent and bills.

She had no idea when this war was going to end, and she would be reunited with her husband.

Unfortunately, because Doris was no longer there to look after the children, she had no choice but to send them away to another family until the war was over.

They went to live on a farm, some miles away, with an elderly couple who had also taken in three other children, who were about the same age as the twins, whose parents were unable to look after them because of the war.

This couple, Fred and Esther, were not very nice people, and they didn't treat the children well at all.

They were made to get up very early in the mornings, to do chores around the farm all day, until bedtime, with very little food.

They were not allowed to play; they were tired and hungry, unwashed and unkempt!

Alfie and Georgie were so very sad because they missed Grandma Doris and their parents.

They didn't know how long they were going to be here at the farm, but it seemed like a very long time!

They could not understand why their little lives had changed so drastically.

When the boys had their fourth birthday, there was no cake or present, no party fun like they had always had…. Instead, they still had to work on the farm.

They lost weight, were dirty, and very, very sad!

Then, one day, a few weeks later, they had just finished feeding the chickens when they looked up and saw their mummy and daddy stood there!

They were so excited that they didn't know what to do… Were they only dreaming?

Soon, they realized it was not a dream; the war was over!!

It was the 8th of May 1944 and the grownups called it VE day!!

The boys were to find out, as they got older, that this meant…

Victory in Europe!

People all over the country were celebrating by having street parties. There were banners and balloons, lots of food and cake and everyone was singing and laughing. Wives were reunited with their husbands, and families were together again after more than four years!!

It was a very happy time indeed. Alfie and Georgie might have been war babies, but they survived, and went on to live long, happy and successful lives... but they NEVER forgot Grandma Doris!

The Stray Cat

Written by Patricia Perry

Original idea by Patricia Perry

10th of May 2020

7th week of lockdown

Chapter One:
Dolly

You would think that being a stray cat would be a sad and lonely life!

This was not the case for Tommy, a ginger and white tomcat. He saw it as a life of fun and adventure!

However, this had not always been the case… He was taken from his mummy at 6 weeks old, and went to live with a sweet old lady called Dolly!

Her real name was Dorothy, but because she had always been a tiny little thing, she was nicknamed Dolly.

Dolly had never married, nor had she ever had a child, but she always had a cat!

Tommy was not her first cat; she had many over the years, and she loved them all but Tommy was her favourite!!

They lived happily together, until one sad day, Dolly died.

When they came to take Dolly away, Tommy heard the men talking about who was going to take the cat.

Tommy's ears pricked up at hearing this, and he thought, 'No-one is going to TAKE ME!'

He'd had a good life with Dolly for seven years, but now he was old enough to make his own way in the big wide world!

He would never forget Dolly; she had been very kind and treated him well.

Chapter Two:
Elsie

For the first few weeks, life felt very strange for Tommy.

He had always been allowed outdoors, as he was not an indoor cat, but after his little wander around, he would always go back home.

Now, he realised, he didn't have a home to go back to.

He had been living on mice and birds and drinking rainwater.

This wasn't too bad at first, but then he began to yearn for his first mistress, Dolly, and the lovely food she gave him, like chicken and tuna, followed by a saucer of milk or cream….

He was feeling a little sorry for himself. He looked bedraggled, and was in dire need of a little love and affection!

Then, one day, after he had been wandering on and on and didn't know where he was, he ended up sitting on the wall outside the house of an elderly lady called Elsie.

Now, as it happened, Elsie lived on her own.

She hadn't always been on her own; she had been married to Freddie for nearly 50 years, but sadly, he had passed away…

Elsie and Freddie had four children, but they were all grown up now and had busy lives of their own!

Elsie had always loved cats, so, when she spotted Tommy on her wall, looking over so sadly, she beckoned him over with a saucer of milk!

Tommy was very excited; it had been so long….

When Elsie opened a tin of tuna for him, it was like a magnificent feast!

After he had been fed and watered, he expected to be shown the door, but, to his surprise, Elsie fussed over him, showing him lots of love, the love he hadn't realised he'd missed so much… He began to purr away, and wag his tail in happiness!

He loved and enjoyed his freedom, but also loved the comforts of home life!

It would be wonderful if he was allowed to go off on his adventures but then return to Elsie for proper food like lamb, chicken and tuna, and some love and cuddles. That would be the perfect life, just like it had been with his first mistress, his beloved Dolly!

Well, much to his joy and surprise, this did happen!

He would sit at the door when he needed to go out… It didn't matter how long he was away for; it could have been days or even weeks.

He never gave a thought that Elsie may be sad and lonely and missed him.

Whenever he returned, she would always be very excited. She would feed him well and have lots of cuddles, and she would even say, "I love you very much," to which Tommy would reply by snuggling up on her lap, gently wagging his tail, and purring!

This was the life!!

This went on for a couple of years, but one day, when he returned after a couple of weeks of chasing rabbits and birds and doing whatever he liked, he was sitting at Elsie's door waiting for the usual welcome, only it didn't happen… He was to learn why a day or two later!

The same men in black suits, with big black cars, took Elsie away, just as they had done with Dolly, never to return!

It suddenly occurred to Tommy that he would miss Elsie terribly, and realised just how selfish he had been, leaving her sad and lonely for weeks on end!!!

Chapter Three:
Matilda

Tommy did not know how long he had been wandering, but I guess now he was classed as a stray cat!

He still grieved his two previous mistresses, Dolly and Elsie, and would never forgive himself for being so thoughtless and selfish…

Why, he wondered, did old people go away with the men in black, never to return home again?

After all, he was just a cat; he didn't know about the circle of life!

One day, he stopped for a rest in the park. He was busy watching a little girl called Matilda happily playing on the slide and swings.

She was having so much fun that it made Tommy happy too!

So, every day for a fortnight, Tommy would go back to the park in the hope of seeing Matilda again, which he did!

It turned out that her mummy took her to the park every morning for fresh air and exercise.

Then one day, Tommy decided to follow them home to see what would happen….

He expected to get shooed away, but they allowed him to follow.

When they arrived home, Matilda said, "Look, Mummy, this lovely cat has been at the park watching us every day, and now he's followed us home. Do you think he's a stray?"

Matilda's mum answered, "Yes, I think he must be. Let's give him some food and milk and see what he does!"

Well, this surprised Tommy even more, as he didn't expect to get fed as well!

Afterwards, they allowed Tommy to remain in the garden. They fully expected him to go away, never to be seen again.

However, Tommy thought differently. If he was to be given another chance of a good home, he was going to take it!

His wandering days were over. He wanted, NEEDED, to give these lovely people as much love and happiness as he could give them!

So, that was his goal; he loved Matilda with all his heart, and, he thought, because she is a little girl, she wasn't going to go away with the men in black, never to return!

They had lots of cuddles and fun together. He never knew this life was just as good, if not better than chasing rabbits…

When Matilda started school, Tommy would follow and wait until she'd gone inside, then was always back there to meet her when school came out at 3 o'clock!

They would play and have fun until bedtime….

Tommy even had his own luxury cat bed!

'This beats sleeping in gardens and sheds,' he thought.

Yes, life was very good indeed.

Then, one day, a couple of years later, when Tommy was nearly 11 years old, Matilda came downstairs after getting ready for school, and expected Tommy to come running to greet her as usual…

But Tommy stayed in his bed. He just looked as if he was asleep, but he would never wake up again.

He had gone to be with his beloved mistresses, Dolly and Elsie, in heaven.

Matilda would NEVER forget Tommy, nor would she ever replace him. He was, and always will be, the BEST cat ever!!

The Favourite Chair

Written by Patricia Perry

An original idea by Jayne Gleaves

Help, support and encouragement from husband Roy Perry

7th of May 2020

7th week of lockdown

Enjoy!!!

Chapter One:
Grandpa Joe

66-year-old Grandpa Joe sat back in his favourite chair, a mahogany leather chesterfield rocker, and admired his handiwork.

He had just finished working in his beautiful garden.

It was his pride and joy!

He had mowed the lawn to perfection. He had gorgeous flower beds, with an array of different coloured blooms and a lovely rose tree in the corner.

His wife, 64-year-old Doris, was indoors cooking his favourite food.

He adored Doris; they had got married 44 years ago, when he was a mere 22 years old, and Doris just 20!

Joe had been lucky in life…

He had a good and happy childhood, even though he was one of six siblings.

His mum and dad, John and Annie, worked very hard to keep their children well-fed and dressed, albeit, it was first up, best dressed!

They were taught respect and manners. Annie would always say, 'respect and manners cost nowt but meant a lot'! They knew right from wrong from a very early age.

Joe was hoping he had done the same, or near enough, for his own two children.

Joe and Doris had two children; a son, Harry, and a daughter, Claire.

Harry was 42 years old and had given Joe two gorgeous grandchildren, 18-year-old Jack, who was about to go off to uni, and 14-year-old Molly.

Their daughter, Claire, had one daughter. She often said, 'that's quite enough thank-you'!! She was called Becky. She was 21 years old, and training to be a doctor.

All in all, Joe considered himself to be a very fortunate man, as he rocked away in his favourite chair!

The chair had belonged to his father, John, who had many years of pleasure in it, until one day, he passed away aged 87, whilst gently rocking in the chair.... He simply fell asleep and never woke up.

It was a great shock to the family, but especially Annie. She was so sad and lonely without John that she passed away a few weeks later. Some would say she died of a broken heart.

That's how Grandpa Joe came to own the chair. It was the only thing he'd wanted, and that's because he knew how much he had loved it!

Joe's wife, Doris, would polish the mahogany chair until it shone... If her Joe was happy, then so was she!

They both had many blessings to count.

Chapter Two:
Grandma Doris

Sadly, Doris did not have the happy childhood that Joe had done.

She was an only child, and her mum, Flo, a lovely lady, had died when Doris was only 14 years old.

A year later, Doris's father married again, this time to a very unpleasant woman called Elsie.

Elsie already had four children, so she had no interest at all in Doris and treated her very unkindly!

Eventually, things got so bad that she left home. It wasn't that she didn't love her dad, but she was so unhappy that she had to leave.

She got a job in a hospital, doing cleaning and general chores. She received a small wage and had a room to live in, provided by the hospital.

So, she had her own freedom and independence.

She worked very hard, but in her spare time, she would go dancing!

Doris absolutely adored her dancing, and it was here that she met Joe… They hit it off almost immediately, and had a lovely courtship, until they wed when Doris was 20 years old.

It was the best thing she could have done.

With Joe's good job on the railways and her job at the hospital, they managed to buy their own home!

This was to bring them both endless years of pleasure, especially the garden, which was Joe's pride and joy!

The Peg Story

Written by Patricia Perry

Original idea by Daniel Logan

Extra ideas and input by Roy Perry

Sat 2nd of May 2020
During lockdown

Enjoy!!!

Chapter One:
The Peg Story

It was late autumn and the nights were drawing in; leaves had fallen and it was cold, wet and windy!

At the end of the washing line, in Mary's back garden hung Mr Peg, looking very sad and forlorn!

As he hung there with his two remaining friends, (there were a dozen in the beginning), he began to reflect on his life.

Pegs have been around since 1853, doing a great service to most households by gripping hold of whatever was necessary, even the largest, heaviest of items, in order for them to blow in the breeze until they were dry!

When Mary first bought her dozen new pegs, she would store them in a pretty peg bag with butterflies on, to keep them clean and happy!

This is when Mr Peg was at his happiest. He even married Mrs Peg, and they were very happy together for many years until Mrs Peg snapped!

As she was no longer able to grip washing, she was thrown into the dustbin!

It broke Mr Peg's heart at first, but then he realised he still had a job to do, so, he carried bravely on, gripping the best he could; after all, he still had his other ten friends.

However, Mary had stopped storing them in the pretty peg bag, and they were left outside on the line!

"Do you think I could have them if you don't use them anymore?" asked Agnes.

Mr Peg, Fred and Joe couldn't stop smiling; they had always loved Agnes, and now they were going to her washing line!

They were so happy; they had been through a lot together…

Now, to their surprise, they did not go on Agnes's line…

She took them home and gave them a good clean… after all, they had been on Mary's line for so long that they were grubby, but still in working order!

Then, instead of going on the line, she put them in her pretty peg bag, along with some other wooden pegs, and hung it up in her lovely warm kitchen!

They had been given a new lease of life. They were warm and cosy and Agnes's kitchen had delicious smells from her cooking and freshly baked bread!

Mr Peg, Fred and Joe could not have been happier, especially when they were taken out into the sunshine to do what they were made to do…

They would grip the clothes fiercely for Agnes until they were dry! HAPPY DAYS!!

Chapter Three:
The Final Days

Agnes was a sweet, kind and caring old lady, who would do anything for anyone.

Mr Peg and his two friends loved her very much indeed.

They were comfortable, happy and content, but alas, they didn't realise that the end was near!

A few months later, on a Sunday morning, Agnes did not come downstairs for breakfast.

Her lovely teapot, with its tea cosy, her cup and saucer, prepared the night before as she always did, remained on the table, untouched, for two days!

Mr Peg, in his wisdom, knew something sad was going to happen.

On the Tuesday, two men in black suits came and took Agnes away in a big black car.

He knew then, they were never going to see their beloved Agnes ever again…

Mr Peg, Fred and Joe, along with the other wooden pegs that they had got to know and like, were never going to be happy again!

A few weeks later, the house was taken over by a young couple called Katie and Alfie…

They were lovely people, but with new ideas; out with the old and in with the new, was the motto!

One day, builders came in and began to rip out Agnes's old kitchen. The teapot and cosy, matching cups, saucers, milk jug and sugar bowl and lots of other items were boxed up and sent to charity shops…

Still, the pretty bag hung on the pantry door.

Mr Peg and his pals wondered every day if this was their last day!

The new modern kitchen was taking shape, with new up to date appliances, which looked very nice.

Then, one day, a large box arrived, containing a new-fangled TUMBLE DRYER!!!

Mr Peg's worst fears were about to happen… They were no longer needed!!

A few days later, after all the pegs had said their goodbyes, the line was cut down to make room for a small extension which they called a "utility room".

Mr Peg, Fred and Joe, and all the others in their pretty peg bag were thrown away, never to be seen again!!